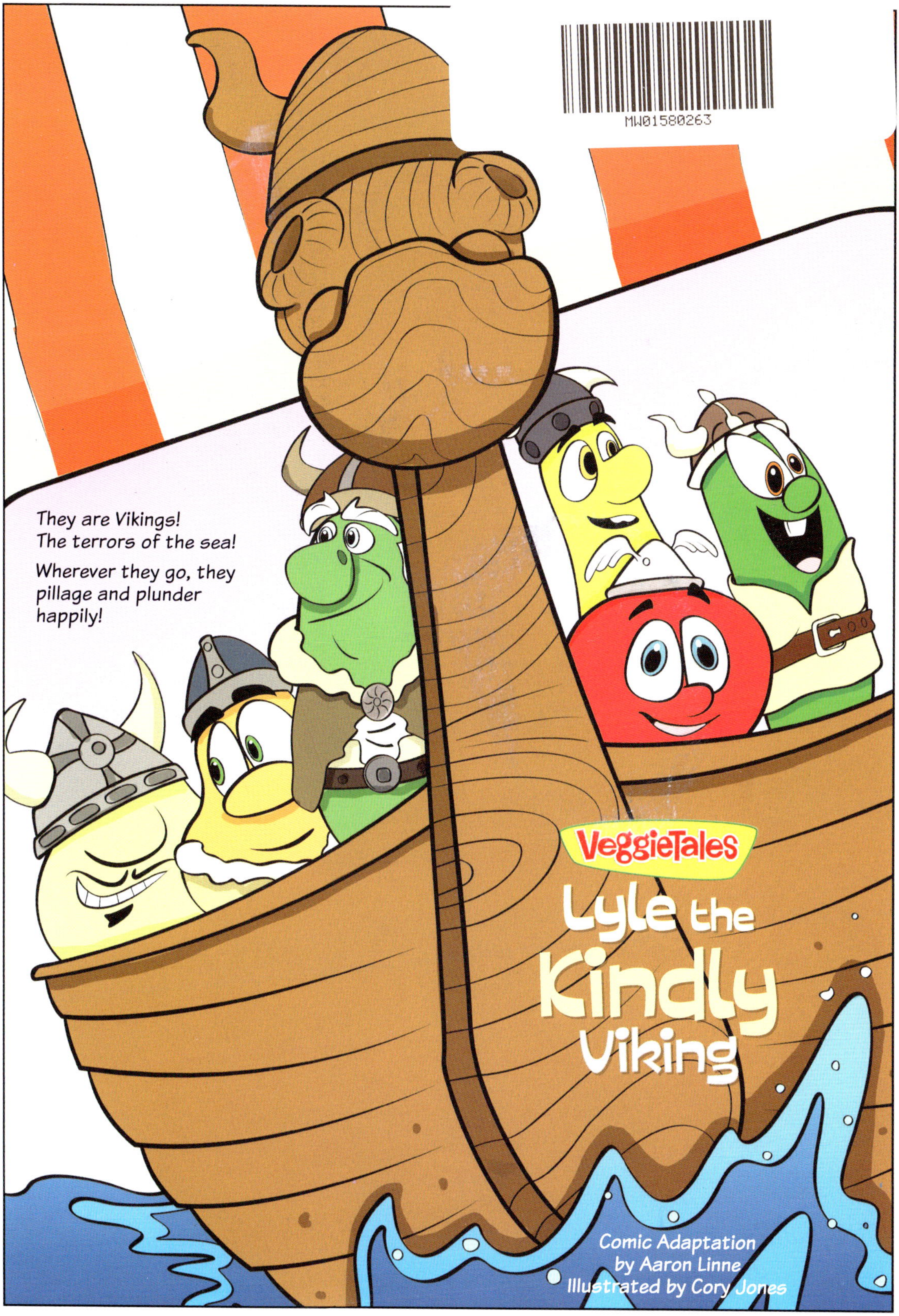
They are Vikings!
The terrors of the sea!
Wherever they go, they pillage and plunder happily!
VeggieTales
Lyle the Kindly Viking
Comic Adaptation
by Aaron Linne
Illustrated by Cory Jones

Being a Viking! Isn't it a hoot?
We take whatever we want— goods, jewels, a big pile of loot!
I even got a giant TV to boot!
Welcome home!

There was one Viking named Lyle who was very different than the rest. He never went on the raids to steal things like the other Vikings.
You missed another raid, Lyle.
I know, I was making stuff.
What was so important that you had to stay here to make it?
Potholders.
Potholders?
Yes, potholders! Would you like one?
No, Lyle, I do not want your silly potholders.
Suit yourself!

Here's your share of the loot, Lyle! Don't worry. It is, in fact, the least we could give you.
Thanks, Harold!
Where are you going now, Lyle? We just got back.
Oh, you know! Places to go, people to see. Bye! I'll be back soon!

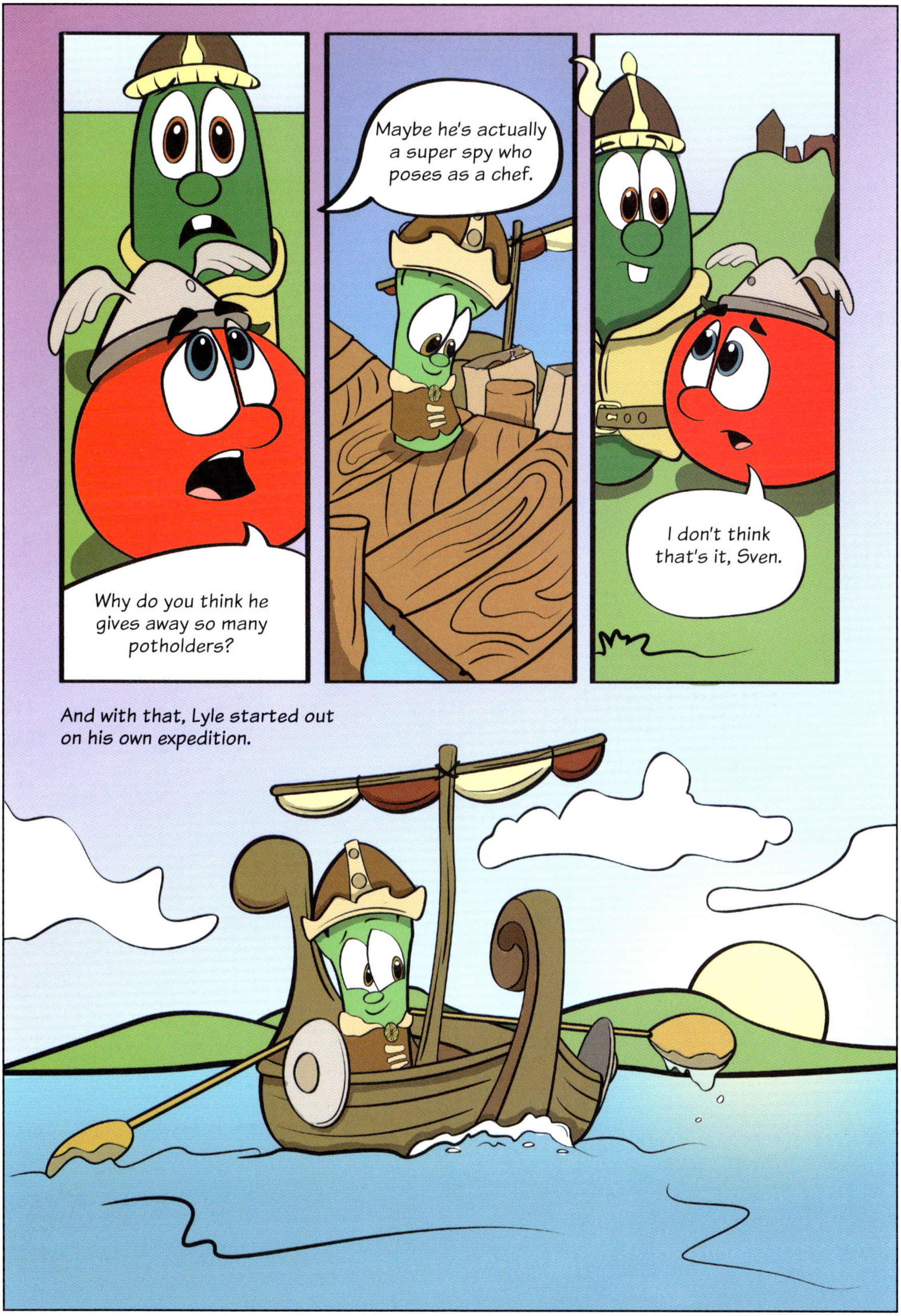
Why do you think he gives away so many potholders?
Maybe he's actually a super spy who poses as a chef.
I don't think that's it, Sven.
And with that, Lyle started out on his own expedition.

What is up with Lyle? He is making me quite distressed.
Why is this boy disrupting our ways? Since 1793 our strategy has been clear—go get stuff from over there and bring it over here! It's always worked for us and gotten us everything we've ever wanted. Why, I have 13 TVs! Where is he going now? Why does he go alone? WHAT'S UP WITH LYLE?

Olaf seems really worried about Lyle, doesn't he?
Yeah, pretty mad too. This could be bad for Lyle.
Should we follow him and make sure he doesn't get into any trouble?
Sure! And maybe see if he has any potholders in green!

We must be in super stealth mode if we're going to follow him.
I'm pretty sure we're close enough.
He's just right there! On the other side of the page!

You're too close.
Now we're too far!
He's getting too far away!
Ok, you've made your point.

He's going back to the monastery we just raided!
Well, it IS the only monastery in the neighborhood.

Dear monks, what can I do? I'm just a small guy, and the other Vikings are so much bigger than me.
But I've brought back what little I have to share with you! It's the least I could do.
Oh, and I made you some potholders.
Potholders? Well, it's the thought that counts.

Dear Lyle, we really do like your style.
We were all despairing, but you rowed your boat all the way here for sharing!
We are no longer blue—and someday we will help you too!
And so, having shared his portion of the loot with the monks, Lyle returned home, happy he could help.

Lyle, you have some explaining to do!
We Vikings rule the seas, we never say please, and we never give stuff back!
So, um . . . why did you give your loot back?
And really, what's up with the potholders?
You both care about your share of gold, right?
And big TVs!
What I care about isn't gold, or money, or even making the coolest potholders in town. What I care about is sharing!

When I share, I get more than just stuff! I get my share of friends too!
You care about having friends?
Yeah! Sharing with friends is the coolest! Like you guys. You're my best friends!
We are?
Yeah! You look out for me. And you've asked me about my potholders more than any other Viking.
I still don't think I understand.
Maybe we should keep this sharing thing our little secret for now. I don't think the other Vikings would understand.
Thanks, guys! You're the greatest!

The next week, during yet another raid on the local monastery . . .
OH, NO
It's Lyle with the monks!
Hurry! We must distract Olaf!

We've got to distract him!
Is that a pterodactyl?
I didn't know pigs played the banjo.

Oh look . . . a whale.
This is really getting weird.
Look anywhere but there!

WHY, THAT LITTLE LYLE IS IN BIG TROUBLE!
He left something with those monks—it's potholders! And that bag of loot we gave him!

CRASH!
What do you think you're doing giving them stuff back?
They're my friends. I just wanted to share with them.
WE'RE VIKINGS! WE. DON'T. SHARE.

Olaf!
You're on your own now, Lyle.
Olaf! The storm! We've got to get out of here!
WE'RE VIKINGS! THE TERROR OF THE SEAS!
Go share with someone else, and see what good it does you!

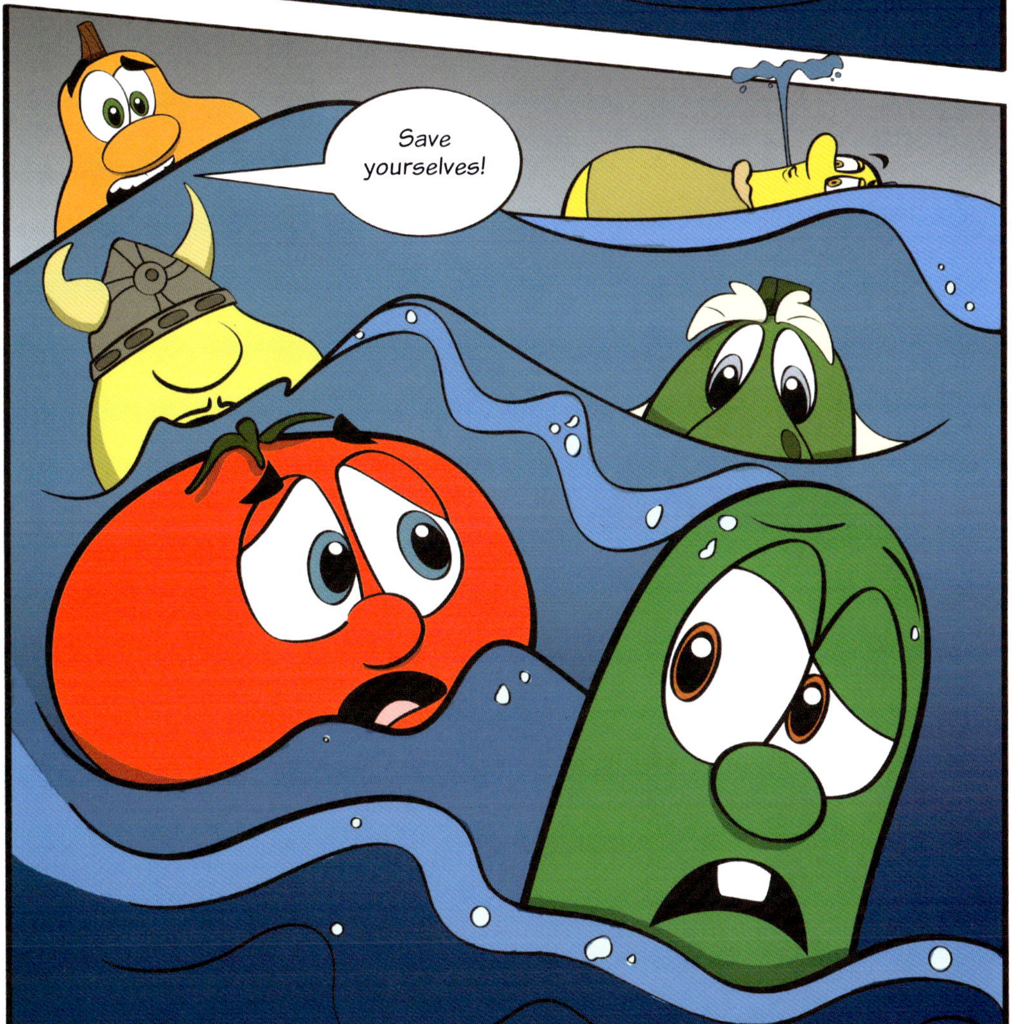
Save yourselves!

Help!!!

Oh no! Look! Lyle has gone overboard!
WE MUST SAVE HIM!
HELP!
Help is on the way, young friend!

Catch!
I don't think that's going to work!
Hey look! A conveniently located life preserver! This should do the trick!
Try again!

I got it!
Thanks, guys!
With all you've done for us, it's truly the least we could do for you!
You can use these potholders to dry off!

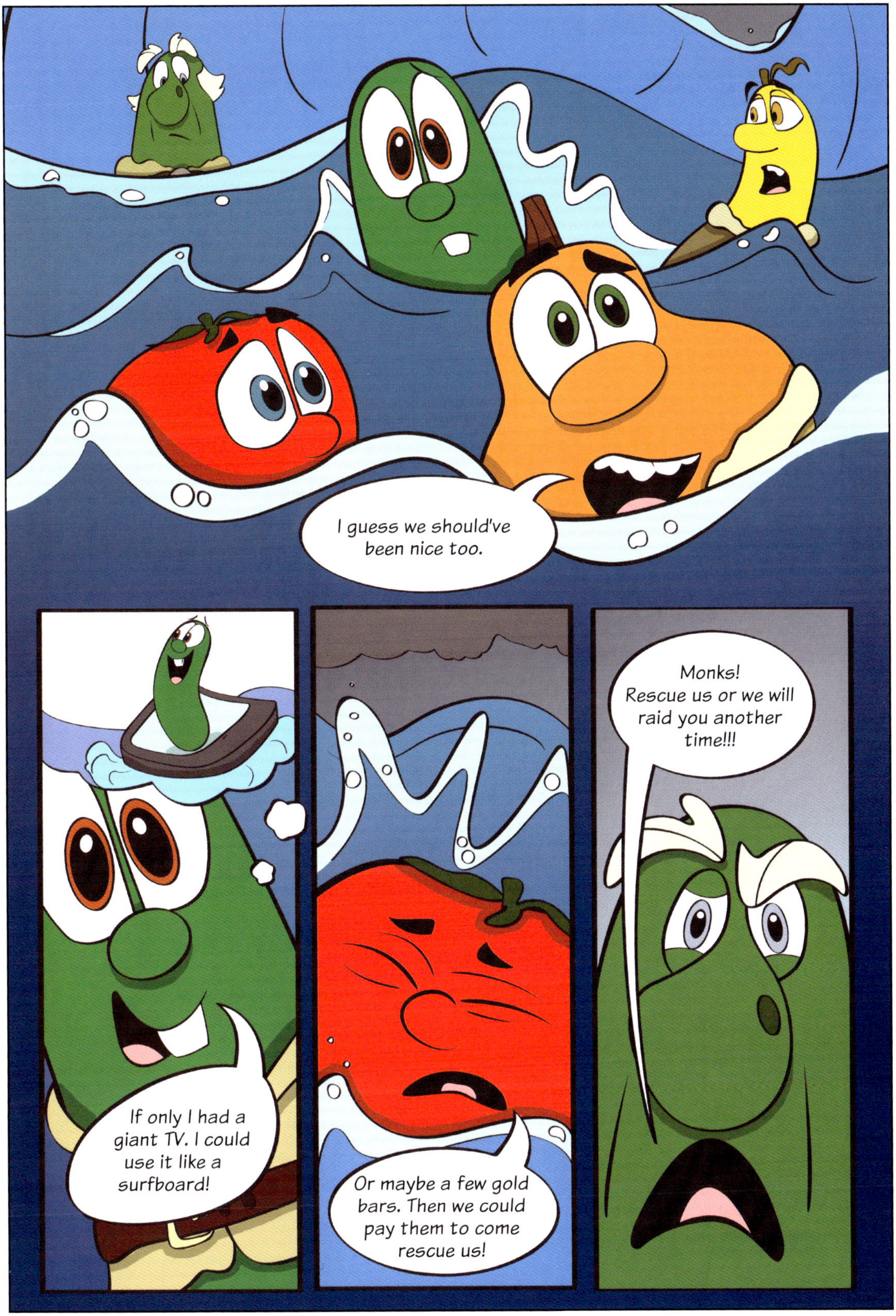
I guess we should've been nice too.
If only I had a giant TV. I could use it like a surfboard!
Or maybe a few gold bars. Then we could pay them to come rescue us!
Monks! Rescue us or we will raid you another time!!!

Now we've got to save the rest of the Vikings!
I don't know, Lyle. They haven't been very nice to us. Every time they come to visit, it's really just to raid and plunder our stuff. We don't think they like us.
I'm pretty sure God wants us to be nice to everyone. Even if they don't like us!
Yeah, we should've known that. We are monks, after all.

Is that for us?
Of course it is! Grab on, and we'll pull you in!

What about me? I don't want to be alone in the sea!
Ok, everybody! He's big. It's going to take all our strength!
WE DID IT!

Thank you, new friends! Your kindness has saved us all.
We'll have a feast to celebrate!
Ohhh! We'll get to use the potholders!
Thanks for sharing, Lyle!
Yeah! Without you, we wouldn't have made so many new friends!
It's like I always say, when we share, we get our share of friends!

We're Vikings!
The sharers of the sea!
And do not forget to do good and to share with others,
for with such sacrifices God is pleased.—Hebrews 13:16 NIV